to --------------------------

with lots of love from

----

and
Mimi
xxx

To Miranda, Ben and Tim - with love

D. S.

ORCHARD BOOKS
338 Euston Road, London NW1 3BH
Orchard Books Australia
Hachette Children's Books
Level 17/207 Kent Street, Sydney, NSW 2000
First published in Great Britain in 2002
First paperback publication in 2004
ISBN 1 84121 350 0 (hardback)
ISBN 1 84362 686 1 (paperback)
Text and illustrations © Daryl Stevenson 2002
The right of Daryl Stevenson to be identified as the author
and illustrator of this work has been asserted by her in accordance
with the Copyright, Designs and Patents Act, 1988.
A CIP catalogue record for this book is available from the British Library.
(hardback) 10 9 8 7 6 5 4 3 2 1
(paperback) 10 9 8 7 6 5 4 3
Printed in Singapore

Mimi's Magic Wardrobe

The Dancing Dress

by Daryl Stevenson

ORCHARD BOOKS

It all began one winter's morning . . .

Mimi awoke knowing somehow that this was going
to be a very special day. With a squeal of delight,
she leapt out of her little bed and threw back the
curtains. What a spectacular sight! Snow had been
falling steadily all night and glistened like millions
of tiny diamonds in the early morning sunshine.
It was so beautiful it quite took
Mimi's breath away.

She hurried downstairs . . .

After some extremely yummy toasted muffins, dripping with honey, and a tiny pot of rosehip tea, Mimi wrapped herself up in her warmest winter coat and spent the entire morning building a big snowmouse!

Later in the afternoon, the snow began to fall very heavily. Mimi curled up on the window seat to watch. It was enchanting to see the millions of tiny flakes swirling and whirling outside, but it meant staying indoors by the fire . . .

"Oh dear," sighed Mimi, "what am I going to do?"
Just then, she felt a gentle breeze around her and
a fluttering of tiny wings. There, hovering above
Mimi's head, was Airy Fairy - Mimi's very
own minuscule fairy godmother!

Airy Fairy waved her magic wand and a tiny
golden key appeared in Mimi's hand.
"Where did this come from?" exclaimed Mimi.
"What might it unlock?"

Off she flew, in and out of every room, trying
the key in cupboards and chests. Down into the cellar
she hurried, and right up to the dusty old attic
which no one had visited for years.

There, at the back of the attic, huddled beneath
the eaves, was a little blue wardrobe. Mimi tried the key.
The wardrobe began to twinkle and shimmer! Carefully,
she opened the door, and there inside was . . .

the MOST exquisite dancing dress!
It was made of delicate pink silk, tied with
a purple sash. "Oh," cried Mimi. "How beautiful!"

Off came Mimi's old dress and on went the new!
She twirled round. It was a perfect fit. It must have
been made especially for her! Then she noticed a pair
of pink ballet shoes and a note saying:

Step
into
the
wardrobe...

Mimi stepped in. The wardrobe
doors gently closed behind her and
then it began to spin round,
faster and faster!

Finally it stopped, the doors opened
and, as she peered out, she found that
she was no longer in the attic.
But if this wasn't the attic,
where was she?

Before Mimi had time to think, a very large
and busy person came rushing up to her.
"Ah, Mimi," she warbled in a strong French accent,
"where 'av you been? I 'av been most anxious.
It iz almost time, quickly my precious."

Suddenly, Mimi was being ushered along
winding corridors until Madame Frou Frou
(for that was the lady's name) was quite out of breath.
She huffed and puffed along, pulling Mimi behind
her, the heels of her elegant red shoes
clackerty-clacking on the floorboards.

Finally, they stopped in the wings of a very large stage. Mimi could see many ballerinas dancing before a large audience. "Oh," gasped Mimi, "it's the Royal Ballet performing Sleeping Beauty, and there's the Queen in her royal box. How WONDERFUL!"

Madame Frou Frou started again in a loud whisper.

"I was so worried my little petit pois.

I nearly 'av an 'art attack, you dizappear like

zis when you are about to go on ze stage.

Tut, tut, zut alors!"

"Go on ze stage!" This dear lady was obviously in dire need of a pair of spectacles and had mistaken Mimi for the lead ballerina. Mimi was just about to explain the mistake when . . . "It iz time, dance like an angel darleeng . . ." with a kiss and a hug, Mimi was given a little shove and there she was, on the stage!

Mimi froze. The spotlight beamed down upon her,
her heart pounded, the orchestra waited,
the audience held its breath . . .

Suddenly, Mimi's feet began to move
and, without knowing how, she danced
like she had never danced before,
twirling and whirling and flying
over the stage as though her
feet had wings!

When she reached the end, everyone stood up, clapping

and cheering. It was the best performance they had

ever seen! Mimi bowed, and bowed again, and proudly

collected bouquets of flowers as Madame Frou Frou

wept with joy in the wings, and then . . .

the strangest thing happened.
Mimi was in the wardrobe
spinning round, faster
and faster until . . .

suddenly it stopped. Mimi was back in
the attic. What an adventure! Carefully, she hung
up the dancing dress, closed the wardrobe doors
and, after turning the golden key in the lock,
she slipped it back into its velvet pouch in
her pocket for safe-keeping . . .

until her next adventure in the magic wardrobe.

Here are some more magical stories from Orchard Books for you to enjoy!

1 84121 296 2

£5.99

" . . . a whimsical story . . . made memorable by Jane Ray's exquisite and atmospheric illustrations."

Carousel

£5.99

1 84121 108 7

"Painted in slabs of glowing colour, with added glitter on the cover, this atmospheric picture book mixes dream with reality in a memorable style all of its own."

Carousel

Orchard paperbacks are available from all good bookshops, or can be ordered direct from the publisher:
Orchard Books, PO BOX 29, Douglas IM99 1BQ
Credit card orders please telephone: 01624 836000 or fax: 01624 837033.
Visit our internet site www.wattspub.co.uk or e-mail: bookshop@enterprise.net for details. To order − please quote title, author and ISBN and your full name and address. Cheques and postal orders should be made payable to 'Bookpost plc'.
Postage and packing is FREE within the UK (overseas customers should add £1.00 per book).
Prices and availability are subject to change.

It was just an ordinary wardrobe, tucked
away in a dusty corner of the attic . . .

That is until Mimi turns the special key
in the lock. Then this rickety old
piece of furniture becomes
Mimi's Magic Wardrobe,
opening a wonderful world
of exciting adventures.

Where will the magic lead?

Lift-the-
flap
finale!

£4.99

ISBN 1-84362-686-1

9 781843 626862